DAY ONE

Akiak knew it. The other dogs knew it, too.

Some had run it many times and others had never run it at all. But not a dog wanted to be left behind.

AKIAK

A TALE FROM THE IDITAROD

Robert J. Blake

Philomel Books · New York

It was Iditarod Race Day. 1,151 miles of wind, snow, and rugged trail lay ahead, from Anchorage to Nome. Akiak had led the team through seven races and knew the trail better than any dog. She had brought them in fifth, third, and second, but had never won. She was ten years old now. This was her last chance. Now, they must win now.

Crack! The race was under way. One by one, fifty-eight teams took off for Nome.

DAY TWO

"Come on, old girl, show 'em how," Mick called. "Haw!"

Mick worked the sixteen-dog team through Akiak, calling "Haw!" when she needed the dogs to turn left, and "Gee!" to go right. Mick was the musher, but the team followed the lead dog. The team followed Akiak.

Through steep climbs and dangerous descents, icy waters and confusing trails, Akiak always found the safest and fastest way. She never got lost.

DAY THREE

Akiak and Squinty, Big Boy and Flinty, Roscoe and the rest of the team pounded across the snow for three days. The dogs were ready to break out, but Mick held them back. There was a right time—but not yet.

High in the Alaskan range they caught up to Willy Ketcham in third place. It was his team that had beaten them by just one minute last year. Following the rules, Willy pulled over and allowed Mick's team to pass.

"That old dog will never make it!" he laughed at Akiak across the biting wind.

"She'll be waiting for you at Nome!" Mick vowed.

DAY FOUR

High in the Kuskokwim Mountains they passed Tall Tim
Broonzy's team and moved into second place. Just after Takotna,
Mick's team made its move. They raced by Whistlin' Perry's
team to take over first place.

Ketcham made his move, too. His team clung to Mick's like
a shadow.

Akiak and her team now had to break trail through deep
snow. It was tough going. By the Ophir checkpoint, Akiak was
limping. The deep snow had jammed up one of her pawpads and
made it sore. Mick tended to her as Ketcham raced by and took
first place from them.

"You can't run on that paw, old girl," Mick said to her. "With
a day's rest it will heal, but the team can't wait here a day. We've
got to go on without you. You'll be flown home."

Roscoe took Akiak's place at lead.

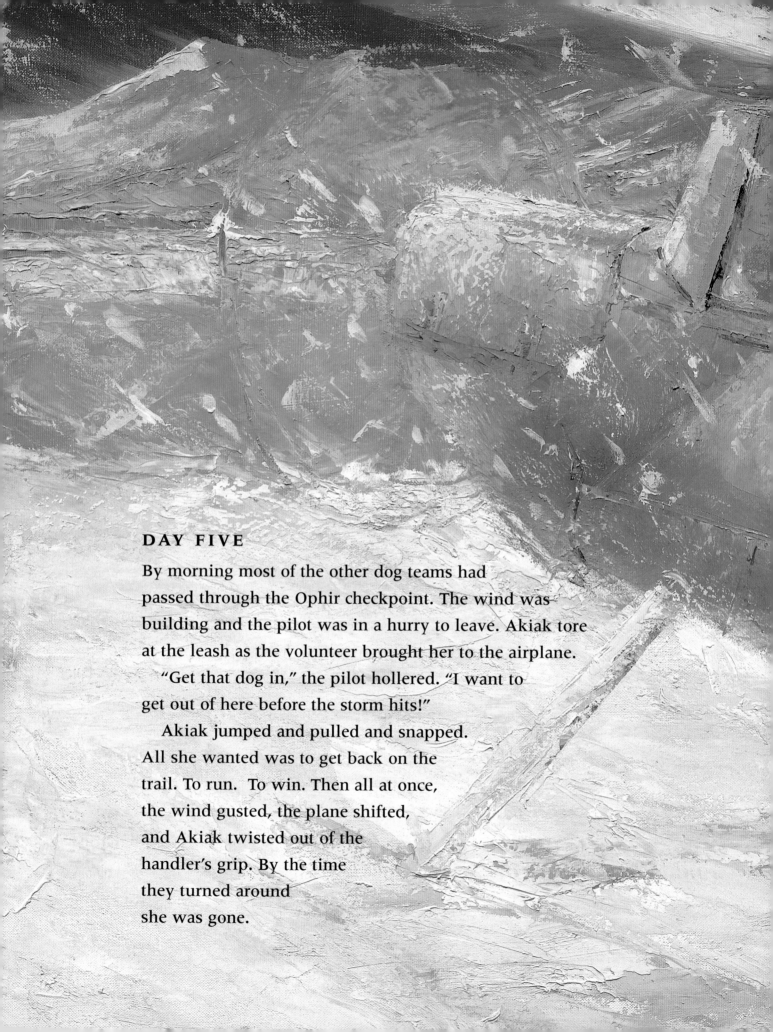

DAY FIVE

By morning most of the other dog teams had
passed through the Ophir checkpoint. The wind was
building and the pilot was in a hurry to leave. Akiak tore
at the leash as the volunteer brought her to the airplane.

"Get that dog in," the pilot hollered. "I want to
get out of here before the storm hits!"

Akiak jumped and pulled and snapped.
All she wanted was to get back on the
trail. To run. To win. Then all at once,
the wind gusted, the plane shifted,
and Akiak twisted out of the
handler's grip. By the time
they turned around
she was gone.

DAY SIX

Akiak ran while the storm became a blizzard. She knew that Mick and the team were somewhere ahead of her. The wind took away the scent and the snow took away the trail, but still she knew the way. She ran and she ran, until the blizzard became a whiteout. Then she could run no more. While Mick and the team took refuge in Galena, seven hours ahead, Akiak burrowed into a snowdrift to wait out the storm.

In the morning the mound of snow came alive, and out pushed Akiak.

DAY SEVEN

Word had gone out that Akiak was loose. Trail volunteers knew that an experienced lead dog would stick to the trail. They knew she'd have to come through Unalakleet.

She did. Six hours after Mick and the team had left, Akiak padded softly, cautiously, into the checkpoint. Her ears alert, her wet nose sniffed the air. The team had been there, she could tell.

Suddenly, cabin doors flew open. Five volunteers fanned out and tried to grab her. Akiak zigged around their every zag and took off down the trail.

"Call ahead to Shaktoolik!" a man shouted.

DAY EIGHT

At Shaktoolik, Mick dropped two more dogs and raced out, still six hours ahead of Akiak.

Hungry now—it had been two days since she had eaten—Akiak pounded over the packed trail. For thirst, she drank out of the streams, the ice broken through by the sled teams.

She struggled into Shaktoolik in the late afternoon. Three men spotted her and chased her right into the community hall, where some mushers were sleeping. Tables overturned and coffee went flying. Then one musher opened the back door and she escaped.

"Go find them, girl," he whispered.

At Koyuk, Akiak raided the mushers' discard pile for food. No one came after her. At Elim, people put food out for her. Almost everybody was rooting for Akiak to catch her team.

DAY NINE

Mick rushed into White Mountain
twenty-two minutes behind Ketcham.
Here the teams had to take an eight-hour lay-
over to rest before the final dash for Nome. Mick
dropped Big Boy and put young Comet in his place.
The team was down to eight dogs with seventy-seven
miles to go.

Akiak pushed on. When her team left White Mountain at
6 P.M., Akiak was running through Golovin, just two hours behind.
A crowd lined the trail to watch her run through the town.

DAY TEN

Screaming winds threw bitter cold at the team as they fought their
way along the coast. Then, halfway to the checkpoint called Safety,
they came upon a maze of snowmobile tracks. The lead dogs lost
the trail.

Mick squinted through the snow, looking for a sign.

There. Going right. She recognized Ketcham's trail.

"Gee!" she called. Gee—go right.

But the dogs wouldn't go. They wandered about, tangling up the
lines. Mick straightened them out and worked the team up the hill.
At the top they stopped short. Something was blocking the trail.

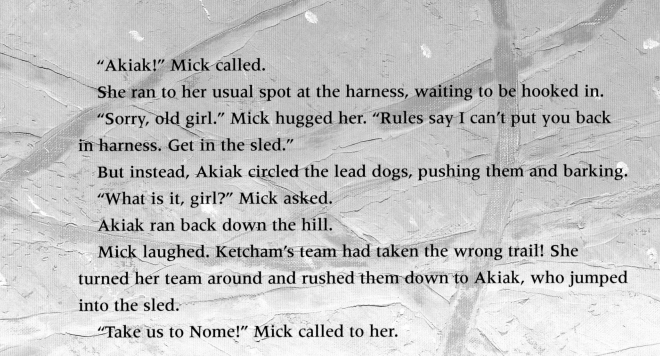

"Akiak!" Mick called.

She ran to her usual spot at the harness, waiting to be hooked in.

"Sorry, old girl." Mick hugged her. "Rules say I can't put you back in harness. Get in the sled."

But instead, Akiak circled the lead dogs, pushing them and barking.

"What is it, girl?" Mick asked.

Akiak ran back down the hill.

Mick laughed. Ketcham's team had taken the wrong trail! She turned her team around and rushed them down to Akiak, who jumped into the sled.

"Take us to Nome!" Mick called to her.

Mick first heard the noise a mile outside of Nome. At first she wasn't sure what it was. It grew so loud that she couldn't hear the dogs. It was a roar, or a rumble—she was so tired after ten days of mushing she couldn't tell which. Then she saw the crowd and she heard their cheers. People had come from everywhere to see the courageous dog that had run the Iditarod trail alone.

As sure as if she had been in the lead position, Akiak won the Iditarod Race.

"Nothing was going to stop this dog from winning," Mick told the crowd. Akiak knew it.

The other dogs knew it, too.

AUTHOR'S NOTE

The Iditarod is, above all, a race of the heart for both human beings and dogs. As with any race, however, the Iditarod has rules to ensure fairness and safety for the mushers and dogs. A musher must stop and sign in at each checkpoint on the trail. In addition, a musher must take a twenty-four-hour stop at some point during the race, one eight-hour stop on the Yukon, and one eight-hour stop at White Mountain. The maximum number of dogs a musher can start with is sixteen. A musher must finish the race with at least five. When one team gets within fifty feet of another, the team behind has the immediate right of way upon demand. The musher ahead must stop his dogs for at least one minute or allow the other team to pass. An injured, sick, or fatigued dog may be dropped at a designated dog drop and flown back to Anchorage to be picked up and taken home. A dropped dog may not be put back in harness and may not run next to the team. However, a loose dog found on the trail may be put in the sled and taken to the next checkpoint.

I would like to acknowledge the hard work and competence of the Iditarod trail volunteers.

—*Robert J. Blake*

For Lynn, with whom I run my race

Many thanks to the following, without whom this book could not have been made: The Iditarod Trail Committee, Joanne Potts, Chrystal Carr Jeter, John Dahlen, Rick Calcote, Susan and Jim Cantor (thanks for getting me on a sled!), Larry Lake (Uncle Animal), Mr. and Mrs. Patsarikas, Mrs. Geitzenaeur, the Chester dojo, Karen Moore, Brian Quinn, and especially, Raven.

Patricia Lee Gauch, editor

Library of Congress Cataloging-in-Publication Data   Blake, Robert J. Akiak: a tale from the Iditarod / by Robert J. Blake, [author and illustrator]. p. cm.   Summary: Akiak the sled dog refuses to give up after being injured during the Iditarod sled dog race. 1. Sled dogs—Juvenile fiction. [1. Sled dogs—Fiction. 2. Dogs—Fiction. 3. Iditarod Trail Sled Dog Race, Alaska—Fiction. 4. Sled dog racing—Fiction. 5. Alaska—Fiction.] I. Title. PZ10.3.B5815Ak 1997 [E]—dc21 97-2251 CIP AC ISBN 0-399-22798-9 10 9 8 7 6 5 4 3 2 1   First Impression

1/98